DOCTOR · WHO

THE DARKSMITH LEGACY

D0553335

BBC CHILDREN'S BOOKS
Published by the Penguin Group
Penguin Books Ltd, 80 Strand, London, WC2R 0RL, England
Penguin Group (USA) Inc., 375 Hudson Street, New York 10014, USA
Penguin Books (Australia) Ltd, 250 Camberwell Road, Camberwell, Victoria 3124, Australia
(A division of Pearson Australia Group Pty Ltd)
Canada, India, New Zealand, South Africa
Published by BBC Children's Books, 2009
Text and design © Children's Character Books, 2009
This edition produced for The Book People Ltd,
Hall Wood Avenue, Haydock, St Helens, WA11 9UL
Written by Justin Richards
Cover illustration by Peter McKinstry
1
ISBN: 9781405906678
Printed in Great Britain by Clays Ltd, St Ives plc

DOCTOR · WHO

THE DARKSMITH LEGACY

THE PLANET OF OBLIVION

BY JUSTIN RICHARDS

Book
7

The Darksmith adventure continues online. Log on to
the website, enter the special codes from your book
and enjoy games and exclusive content about
The Darksmith Legacy.

www.thedarksmithlegacy.com

Contents

The Story So Far...

The Doctor has taken the powerful Eternity Crystal from the terrible Darksmith Collective on the planet Karagula. The Crystal can create life, and the Doctor knows it mustn't be allowed to fall into the wrong hands. The Darksmiths need the Crystal to fulfil their contract to create a device for a mysterious client.

With the help of Gisella – the robotic 'daughter' of Varlos, the Darksmith who created the Crystal – the Doctor tries to find out who the Darksmiths are working for. The people who commissioned the Crystal are the only ones who know how to destroy it.

But all the Doctor and Gisella have to go on is the robotic mind of the powerful Agent the Darksmiths sent after the Doctor to recover the Eternity Crystal…

Arrival

'Standing up to that robot was incredibly brave,' the Doctor told Gisella. 'I couldn't have stopped it on my own – and it's thanks to you that we've now got this.' He tapped the little electronic component.

'The robot's brain? How will that help us?'

'Well it's more of a computer core matrix than a brain, and it shares some of the same crypto-molecular structure as the Eternity Crystal. Which is exactly what the TARDIS needs to work out a way for us to destroy it.'

'Brilliant!'

'Couldn't have put it better myself,' the Doctor said, flipping the sonic screwdriver and catching it with a flourish. 'There – all done.'

The console pulsed with light and the tiny

component sparkled in its nest of wires and circuitry. The Doctor pulled the scanner screen around and tilted it for them both to check the readout.

His face fell. 'Oh dear, that's not good news...'

Gisella watched the hexagonal patterns moving on the screen. She still couldn't work out how to interpret them, but the Doctor was clearly concerned. 'Why? What does it mean?'

'According to the TARDIS, the only people with the power and technology to destroy the Crystal are those who commissioned its creation. A sort of doomsday circuit.'

'And who are they? Who commissioned the Darksmiths originally to create the Eternity Crystal?'

'I haven't a clue. But there is some data embedded deep in this brain that has survived. An appointment, a meeting of some sort. It looks as though a delegation of Darksmiths recently met with their mysterious client to discuss the Eternity Crystal. Probably when they realized it had resurfaced. The co-ordinates refer to a particular planet.'

'Which is?'

The Doctor stared at the screen, his face grim. 'Ursulonamex. Otherwise known as Oblivion.'

'That doesn't sound very nice.'

'No,' agreed the Doctor. 'But you'd be surprised.' He looked thoughtful for a few seconds and then suddenly grinned at her. 'So what are we waiting for?'

And then he threw the lever that would send the TARDIS hurtling through time and space – towards Oblivion.

'Won't take long,' the Doctor assured Gisella. 'Well, I say it won't take long. But long doesn't actually mean anything when we're travelling in the TARDIS. Or short. Or quick or slow or just about ten minutes more or less.'

Gisella laughed. Although she was a robotic android created by the Darksmith Varlos, she looked like a young girl, perhaps eleven years old. She had a very round, pale and delicate face with big, dark eyes and black hair cut in a perfect bob.

Varlos had used the same technology that had created the Eternity Crystal, which the Darksmiths were so desperate to recover, to give Gisella life. She was much more than a robot. For one thing, the Doctor thought, she could laugh.

'I have no idea what you're on about Doctor,' Gisella said. 'You talk such rubbish sometimes.

Why can't you just say what you mean?'

And she could be a bit annoying too – *rubbish*?! The Doctor sighed. 'I mean, that it might not seem like it, but we'll be there in the blink of an eye. A moment after leaving Devastation Hall behind, we'll arrive on Ursulonamex.'

The central column of the TARDIS was rising and falling rhythmically. The sound of the time machine's powerful engines cut through the control room – a rasping, grating noise.

'In fact, here we are,' the Doctor said, running round the console and checking the controls. He paused, frowning as he examined a readout. He picked up a large hammer he kept handy for just this sort of thing, and thumped it down hard on the console. 'There, that's better.'

'Are we there?' Gisella asked.

The Doctor grinned massively. 'Welcome to the Planet of Oblivion.' He reached for the door control.

'So why's it called the Planet of Oblivion?' Gisella asked.

13

TARDIS
Data Bank
The Forests of Ursulonamex

The planet Ursulonamex

The planet Ursulonamex is half ocean and half forest. The oceans are deep and blue, teeming with fish and other marine life. The water is heavily oxygenated and constantly filled with small bubbles. As on the pleasure planet Florana, the bubbles in the water support swimmers so they cannot sink.

The forests too are idyllic by human standards. In places, they are dense enough to cut out sunlight. But there are frequent forest clearings where the twin suns warm the ground, which is covered with exo-pine needles.

The ecosystem is perfectly balanced, the plant life in the forests both emitting and taking carbon dioxide from the atmosphere and maintaining the planet's almost tropical temperature and weather system.

Like the rainforests of Earth, the forests of Ursulonamex are divided into different layers, each with its own plants and animals native to that part of the forest:

- **The Emergent Layer** – Some very tall trees grow higher than the canopy. These are home to high-flying birds like eagles.
- **The Canopy Layer** – As its name suggests, this is the near-complete cover formed by the tops of the trees that touch and overlap each other.
- **The Understory Layer** – This is the area between the forest floor and the tops of the trees (the Canopy layer). Sometimes the lower part of the Understory Layer is called the Shrub layer.
- **The Forest Floor Layer** – This is the ground under the trees. Because there is so little sunlight (except in the clearings, where there is dense undergrowth), only plants that can survive in low light can grow here. As a result, the forest floor is actually almost clear.

The Planet of Oblivion

Ursulonamex has long been a favoured holiday destination. With its lush forests and beautiful oceans, life forms come to the planet to forget their problems. For this reason it is known as *The Planet of Oblivion*. Accommodation is provided in the great Cities of Green – living space made out of the trees themselves. The larger trees are hollowed out and whole rooms created inside. The resulting houses are connected by tree-walks – bridges across branches – and by pathways across the forest floor.

Each City of Green exists in harmony with nature. The trees are never hollowed or cut so much that they die, and saplings can be trained to grow along ropes and up stakes to form the desired shapes and structures.

It was almost dark in the forest. But Gisella's electronic eyes immediately adjusted to the low light. Patches of pale sunlight broke through the canopy of trees and dappled the ground.

'People come here to forget,' the Doctor said. 'They come to leave all their troubles behind and get away from it all. To immerse themselves in the environment. To be at one with nature.' He paused, turning in a full circle as if to get his bearings. 'Can you smell burning?'

Gisella could. Her sense of smell was probably even more accurate than the Doctor's. 'It's coming from that direction.' She pointed in the opposite direction to where the Doctor was facing.

'Just the way I was going,' the Doctor agreed, swinging round. 'And just the way I think we need to go to find the nearest City of Green. The paths all lead that way, look.'

Sure enough, the paths that had been worn on the forest floor did seem to run that way. A second path joined the one they were following a few metres ahead, and another further on still. Beyond that, Gisella could see there was more sunlight.

'We should be able to see where we are from that clearing,' the Doctor said. 'The clearings are all connected by paths, and arranged round the City of Green. They provide light for the houses and dwellings without the need for electricity.'

'Or fire?'

'Yes,' the Doctor said slowly. 'That is a bit worrying.' He sniffed again. 'Oh, it's probably just a barbecue. Nothing to worry about. And as soon as we find someone, we can ask if they've seen any spaceships that look like flying cathedrals and find out what the Darksmiths are up to.'

'That easy?' Gisella asked with a smile.

'Doubt it,' the Doctor was smiling too. 'But it's a start. They try not to use too much advanced technology, but they do have it. There'll be air-traffic control systems, spaceports, tracking satellites, the lot.'

'So someone will know the Darksmiths came here, even if they tried to sneak in and out unobserved when they met with their clients.'

'That's right.'

They had reached the edge of the clearing now. The Doctor was leading the way. The sunlight seemed dazzlingly bright after the gloom of the forest. The clearing was on a slight slope, situated on the side of a hill overlooking the vast stretches of forest below. The Doctor stopped, looking out over the view.

'Then again,' he said quietly. 'Maybe they didn't try to sneak in and out. Maybe they didn't care who saw they were here, because all the time...'

Gisella had joined him, staring down at the same view as the Doctor was seeing.

'Because, all the time,' she finished for him, 'they were planning to destroy anyone and anything that witnessed it.'

Below them, smoke was rising from the burned out husks of blackened trees. The once proud and peaceful City of Green lay in twisted, broken, smoking ruins.

From behind them came the roar of a wild animal. Gisella turned, just in time to see a dark shape launch itself out of the forest and charge straight towards her.

The Survivors

Gisella stood her ground as the animal charged. It was dark grey in colour, a cross between a panther and a wolf. Its massive jaws were dripping with saliva, and its eyes were deep red. Clawed feet scrabbled at the ground as it launched itself towards Gisella.

Of course, she was stronger than she looked. But even so, the weight of the animal would send her flying down the hill. Its claws could shred her body, its teeth could rip her to bits.

At the last moment, she hurled herself to one side. She hoped the animal would keep going – carried over the ridge and down the slope by its own momentum. But it landed on all fours, digging its claws in and turning to face her. Gisella was sprawled on the ground as the animal prepared to charge again.

Then it stopped. Its head tilted to one side, confused.

The Doctor stepped between Gisella and the animal, making encouraging noises. He held out his hand, clicking his fingers.

'Come on, come on. There's a good… thingy.'

For a moment it looked like the animal would calm down and come to the Doctor. Any minute now, Gisella thought, he'll be stroking its back and asking what all the fuss was about.

But then the animal's jaws opened in a vicious snarl, and it was moving again.

'Whoops!' the Doctor said.

He whipped off his coat, holding it with the dark lining facing the charging animal. Gisella scrambled out of the way as the Doctor pulled the coat sideways. The animal charged on, missing the Doctor and his coat.

'Learned that from a famous stevedore,' the Doctor said proudly.

The animal was charging again. The Doctor's grin faded. 'Hang on, a stevedore's someone who works down the docks.' He glanced at Gisella. 'I hope he knew what he was talking about!'

With a roar of anger and a slash of claws, the

animal was flying through the air. The Doctor pulled the coat away again. There was an awful ripping sound. The Doctor fell backwards.

The animal kept flying, tumbling over the ridge. Gisella saw it reach the bottom of the slope. It scrambled back to its feet and glared up at her and the Doctor.

The Doctor waved.

The animal opened its jaws in a final snarl, then limped away across the devastated ground.

'Oh no!' the Doctor's smile was gone. He held up his coat, showing Gisella where the lining had been torn. 'And I just bet there's no tailor down there. Come on.'

It took them an hour to walk down the slope into the ruined forest. As they approached, Gisella saw that some of the low-lying trees and shrubs had survived whatever happened. It looked as if a massive forest fire had torn through the woods as far as they could see.

There were people too. Because their skin was tinged green, and they were wearing brown clothes that seemed to be fashioned from leaves and bark, it was easy to miss them. But they were there –

watching as the Doctor and Gisella walked into the midst of the devastation.

A little boy ran up to them, curious. He looked at the Doctor, then giggled and ran away.

'Friendly chap,' the Doctor said. Louder, he called: 'I'm the Doctor, and this is my friend Gisella. We're here to help – if we can,' he added, looking round at the burned out husks of trees and blackened ground.

'The forests will recover,' a voice said from behind them. 'They always do. Fire clears the dead wood and the old trees and makes room for new life.'

'I like a positive attitude,' the Doctor said as he turned.

The man who had spoken was holding a long stave stripped of bark. There were several other people with him – all of them dressed in the rough, woodland clothing Gisella had noticed before.

'What happened here?' Gisella asked. 'Who did this?'

The man seemed to be spokesman and leader. The others watched him as he answered the question: 'There was a mighty rain of fire from the heavens,' he said. 'For a day and a night, it poured down on us. And not just here. The City of Pine and the City of Birch are gone, just like our home – the City of Oaken Leaves.'

'I'm sorry,' the Doctor said. 'I'm so very sorry. It shouldn't have happened.'

'Was it your fault?' the man asked sharply. 'Have you come here for forgiveness? To confess?'

The Doctor shook his head. 'We're involved, I can't deny that. But we're trying to stop the people who did this to you from ever doing anything like it again.'

'They would do this again?' one of the women said, amazed and appalled.

'Given the chance they'll do far worse. It's up to me and Gisella to make sure they never get that chance. Will you help us?'

'Of course,' the leader said. 'But how can we help? We are a peaceful people, we have no weapons.'

'Oh you've got the greatest weapons of all,' the Doctor told him. 'You've got optimism, you've got knowledge and wisdom.'

The man nodded. 'It takes a wise man to realize that. What can we tell you?'

'We need to know who did this,' Gisella said. 'Where they came from, and where they went to afterwards.'

'When the rain of fire poured down in a mighty torrent,' the man said, 'we knew it came from ships in the sky. High up, above the atmosphere, orbiting our world. We have people who understand such things. Our visitors come from space, they too know these things. Many of us died, but perhaps up in space, some survived in the metal homes.'

'Satellites?' the Doctor said.

The man nodded. 'Stations, they are called. Tracking and organizing the visitors and their skyships. Some may survive.'

'We saw several of the stations explode,' the woman who had spoken before told them.

'The great Cities of Green on the other side of our world survived,' the leader said. 'Or so we are told. News is difficult to come by at the moment, but we have heard from the City of Singing Flowers, and the City of Hornbeams has promised to send us help. So perhaps, up there…' He pointed at the sky.

'Yes,' the Doctor said. 'Perhaps. Thank you.'

'May I ask you something?' the man said.

'Of course.'

'Why?'

'Why?' Gisella echoed, not understanding.

The man raised his at the devastated landscape. 'All this – why? Why did they do it?'

'To keep a secret,' the Doctor said. 'To erase any trace that they were here – who they were or who they met. To hide these things from many people – including us, I'm afraid.' He took the man's hand and griped it tight in friendship and sympathy. 'I am so sorry.'

The man nodded. 'So am I,' he said, and turned away.

They walked back to the TARDIS in silence. Only when they were inside the control room did the Doctor speak.

'That animal that attacked us,' he said. 'The poor creature. It must have been so frightened.'

'I was frightened,' Gisella said. 'But at least I know some of what's going on.'

'Let's fill in the blanks, then,' the Doctor told her. He busied himself at the control console. 'Let's find an orbit station that survived. They'll be networked, so they should have copies of the tracking and surveillance data from all the other stations. Even the ones that aren't there any more.'

'If there are any left,' Gisella said quietly.

Activity

Planet Ursulonamex at Estimated Time of Attack

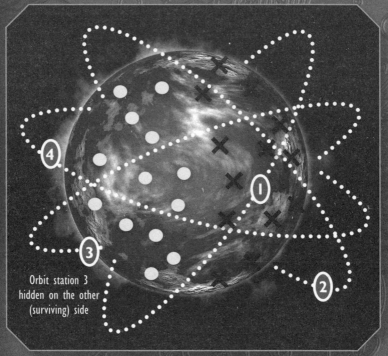

Orbit station 3 hidden on the other (surviving) side

From the extent and position of the destruction of the Cities of Green, work out which Orbit Station is most likely to have survived the attack.

⬤ Cities of Green - Surviving

✖ Cities of Green - Destroyed

◯ Orbit station

Into Orbit

The Doctor and Gisella looked at the scanner. The Doctor tapped on the symbol representing the Orbit Station.

'If any of them survived the attack, it will be that one.'

'Because it was on the far side of the planet when the attack took place.'

The Doctor nodded. 'They devastated this side. Just wiped out the whole of it, to get rid of the one small area they'd visited and where they might have been seen. Very crude but very effective. And very nasty.'

'But Orbit Station 3 was shielded by the planet – like the surviving Cities of Green.'

The Doctor grinned. 'Exactly. It may have been caught in the shock wave, or the attackers might have gone after it anyway as a target. But maybe – just maybe – it's still there.'

'So how do we find out?'

'We go and see.' The Doctor reached for the dematerialization control.

The main docking bay of Orbit Station 3 was a mess. Sections of the wall were blackened and burned. Cables hung broken from the ceiling and junction boxes sparked. Debris was strewn across the floor. The main door into the Orbit Station was jammed open with a metal crate.

The shattered and broken remains of a shuttle craft lay in the middle of the area. Its nose cone had been ripped off and the main engines were a charred mess. It was lying on its side.

In the middle of the chaos, the TARDIS arrived. The sound of its engines broke the silence and it faded into existence close to the wrecked shuttle. The doors opened and the Doctor and Gisella came out.

'Not looking good,' the Doctor said. 'Probably got caught in the shockwave and bashed about rather a lot.

'You think there were survivors?' Gisella asked.

'The air supply is working.' The Doctor jumped up and down a couple of times. 'Gravity is turned on.' He pointed towards the main airlock doors, huge metal plates that held back the vacuum of space. 'There's a ship docked, though I don't recognize the design. Yes,' he decided, 'I think there will be survivors. Let's go and introduce ourselves.'

'And who do we say we are?'

'Oh I don't know. Emergency repair team, perhaps. Insurance assessors come to see the damage. Or a crack team from the beverage vending company come to sort out the coffee machines.'

Outside the docking area, the rest of the Orbit Station was just as damaged. They passed several teams of the green-skinned people working on equipment, or moving debris.

'The attack was a while ago,' the Doctor said. 'So this place must have been in quite a state if they're still clearing up.'

'Can we help?' Gisella asked.

'I expect they know what they're doing. But we'll ask.'

There was a small group of people in overalls working in a room off the corridor. The Doctor walked in, hands deep in his pockets. He looked round with interest.

'Where are we?' Gisella asked, looking at all the damaged equipment and controls.

'Secondary control room. There'll be several of them round the outer hub of the station. It's shaped like a big wheel, with the main control room in the middle, at the hub. Then at intervals round the edge you have these secondary control rooms, each one responsible for a section of the rim. They keep the life support working, make sure the gravity's turned on, maintain the communications network and if you're lucky offer tea and coffee and biscuits.'

'I can't see any tea or coffee or biscuits,' Gisella said, looking round the room.

'I did say, if you're lucky. Guess we're out of luck. Hello there!'

This last greeting was aimed at the man who had come to see what they wanted. He was short and rather fat, with a bald, pale green head that glistened with sweat.

'Can I help you?' the man asked.

'We were just wondering the same thing,' the Doctor told him. 'Weren't we, Gisella? This is Gisella, by the way, and I'm the Doctor, and we were wondering if you need any help with anything. At all.'

'I think we can manage,' the man said. He sounded suspicious. 'I haven't seen you around before.'

'No, no. Just arrived. With the, er – you know.'

'The Dravidians?' the man asked.

The Doctor snapped his fingers. 'The Dravidians.'

'I find that hard to believe.'

'The Dravidians,' the Doctor said again quickly, 'are not the people we came with. Oh no. No, no, no. We're actually with…' He paused, and searched his pockets until he found his wallet of psychic paper. 'Well, you can see for yourself.'

The man peered at the paper. He seemed to stiffen, almost coming to attention. 'Galactic Bureau of Investigation.' He seemed impressed.

'Yeah, GBI. That's us. Agents Doctor and Gisella.' The Doctor glanced at Gisella. 'She's doing work experience,' he explained. 'Very gifted. Older than she looks. Sorry – and you are?'

'Chief Engineer Tyrall, sir.'

'Oh please, don't "sir" me. Just Doctor will do. So, Chief Engineer Tyrall – good job repairing that Altoman Cut-out, by the way,' he said nodding at one of the control panels. 'Excellent job. Anyway, tell us all about it would you. In your own words.'

Tyrall shrugged. 'Not much to tell. The heat-strike took out Stations 1, 2, and 4. Knocked us about rather a lot, as you can see. But the hull stayed secure. We didn't lose air, and we had only minor casualties.'

'Any idea who it was?' Gisella asked.

'The other stations probably got tracking and identity data. We didn't even see them. Which is how we survived the attack, of course.'

'Aren't you networked?' Gisella said, remembering the Doctor's words in the TARDIS. 'Don't you have access to their data?'

'Probably. But the systems are still offline. When we get them running again we can check if they downloaded the data to local storage before the other stations were destroyed. But we've had other priorities.'

'So we see,' the Doctor said. 'Good work.' He pated the man on the shoulder. 'Really good. Thanks for your help, Chief Engineer.'

'No problem.' Tyrall turned back to the team of people working on the repairs. 'Watch it, Karla – not like that. Here, give it to me.' At once he was absorbed in the work again.

The Doctor and Gisella left them to it.

'Let's head for main control,' the Doctor said. 'See if they've got their computers and data storage back online yet.'

They reached a junction. There used to be a sign board on the corridor giving directions to different departments and facilities. But now it was an unreadable, blackened mess.

'That's useful,' the Doctor said. 'This way, I think.' Almost as soon as he'd taken one path, he swung round to head down another. 'This way, I think,' he said again.

As they continued there seemed to be more people at work. Before long they arrived at a large set of double doors. The doors were open, and beyond them, Gisella could see what must be the main control room of the Orbit Station.

It was situated in the middle of the central hub of the wheel-shaped station. Huge windows looked out over the blackness of space. The edge of the planet Ursulonamex was just visible at the bottom of the windows. The oceans were deep blue, and the land looked incredibly green. Gisella remembered that this was the side of the planet that had escaped the worst of the devastating attack.

A tall man with a weather-beaten face that looked

like an old leaf and a shock of very white hair stood in the middle of the vast room. He was obviously in charge, and the Doctor headed straight for him.

The man's eyes narrowed. 'Doctor and Gisella?' he said.

The Doctor and Gisella stopped dead in their tracks.

'Yes,' the Doctor said. 'But, how did you know?'

The man smiled thinly. 'Tyrall called in, said you were on your way. I'm surprised the GBI got agents here so quickly. I'd have sent someone to meet you, but the comms and the surveillance are still out. We literally didn't see you coming, I'm afraid.'

'No problem,' the Doctor assured him. 'It happens.'

'We often turn up sort of unannounced,' Gisella said.

The man reached out to shake hands. 'I'm Commander Sarla. Welcome aboard.'

'Thank you. We're glad to help,' the Doctor said.

'Well, we're obviously grateful for any help we can get. You'll be wanting the surveillance data, I gather. But before that's possible we need to finish the vital repairs.'

But Gisella wasn't listening any more. She was watching in horror over the Commander's shoulder as a creature reared up.

It was an enormous insect – like a grasshopper, with a long body, wide head and huge segmented eyes. Two massive mandibles emerged from the creature's mouth, sharp enough to slice through anything. Thin, spindly forelimbs reached out towards the Commander, claws clicking together as it rose up behind him.

The Dravidians

Gisella grabbed the Doctor's arm. She was about to yell a warning to Commander Sarla.

But the Commander was still speaking: 'Fortunately,' Commander Sarla was saying, 'we have some help already. Let me introduce Hive Captain Mantis.'

He turned towards the creature, which tilted its head slightly to one side and made a high-pitched chittering sound. It took Gisella a moment to realize that the sound was actually speech – the creature was talking to them.

'I am delighted to make the acquaintance of two such noble representatives of the Galactic Bureau of Investigation,' it said. 'My crew and I will of course be happy to offer any and all assistance.'

The Doctor grinned. 'Aw – that's nice. Isn't

that nice, Gisella?'

'We were lucky that the Dravidians were in this sector and picked up our distress calls.'

'Weren't you just.' The Doctor's smile was fixed, and didn't reach his eyes. Gisella wondered what was troubling him. 'So, that was your ship docked to the main airlock, was it?'

The Dravidian inclined its head. 'It was indeed. How kind of you to notice.'

'Hive ship is it?' the Doctor asked. He sounded casual, but Gisella could tell he was paying close attention to the creature's reply.

'Returning from the Hatching World of Slovv. With more Dravidians we could offer more help. But my crew is sadly small.'

Commander Sarla nodded. 'There's just Captain Mantis and his two colleagues. But beggars can't be choosers, and we're happy for any help we can get.'

'I'm sure you are. Can't complain. Make the best of it.' The Doctor smiled up at the Dravidian. 'Like the Commander says, lucky you were around then, wasn't it?'

The Dravidian inclined its head in agreement. 'Fortunate, indeed.'

The Doctor turned back to Commander Sarla.

'Tell you what, why don't Gisella and I take a look at the data systems and keep out of your way. You won't even know we're here. Hive Captain Mantis and his chums can help you with the real work, like...' He paused to lean forward and see what the Dravidian had been working on down by the Commander's feet. 'Like the life support systems. Funny – I thought they were working already.' He took a deep breath. 'So they are. Supporting our lives.'

'Maybe they need checking,' Gisella said.

'They need checking,' the Dravidian captain echoed quickly. 'They could be more efficient, and the station has limited supplies.'

'Of course. Very convincing, don't you think?' the Doctor asked Gisella.

'I'm convinced,' she told him. 'Maybe we should look at the data systems now?'

'I'll get Lieutenant Jagellan to show you what we've got,' Commander Sarla said.

He called over a young woman with dark hair and rather angular, pale green features, and asked her to help the Doctor and Gisella find what they needed.

The data systems were in a small room of their own, off the main control area. Lieutenant Jagellan led the way and showed the Doctor and Gisella the damaged systems.

'I'm afraid they took the shock wave quite badly. We haven't been able to get them back online, and so far no one's had time to look at doing proper repairs.'

'Oh I'm sure we'll manage,' the Doctor told her.

'How long have the Dravidians been here?' Gisella asked.

'A few days. But already they're making a difference. They helped us get the air supply running properly. We had to rely on recycled air until they helped fix it. The oxygen levels reduce with every cycle, and eventually…'

She didn't need to explain further. Gisella knew what would happen. There had been a similar emergency system on the underwater base where she had worked until the Doctor arrived. Eventually the air would have so little oxygen left in it that the crew would suffocate.

'Plenty of oxygen now, that's for sure,' the Doctor said. 'Bit too much if anything.' He took a deep breath. 'I mean – taste that air! That's bracing, that is.'

'They're still working on it,' Jagellan said. 'But better too much oxygen than too little, wouldn't you agree?'

The Doctor nodded. 'Oh yes.'

'So, can I leave you to it?'

'We'll be fine,' Gisella assured her.

Jagellan pointed to another door at the side of the room. 'If you want to take a break or get a drink, the canteen's just through there, down the corridor on the left. Save you coming all the way back through main control.'

'Save us getting in your way, you mean?' the Doctor said.

Jagellan smiled. 'That too,' she admitted. 'You can have too much help sometimes.'

'Don't I know it,' the Doctor said. 'But my help is always a bonus. You might want to ask yourselves what your Dravidian mates are really contributing.'

Gisella waited until Jagellan had gone and they were alone before she asked the Doctor: 'Do you think the Dravidians are up to no good?'

The Doctor clicked his teeth. 'Not sure. They're

a nasty lot, only ever out to help themselves. And I mean help themselves to whatever technology and assets they can find. Like other people's wealth, planets, orbit stations…'

'Then we should warn Commander Sarla.'

'They do seem to be helping, though,' the Doctor went on. 'So maybe I'm thinking of how they were in the past. Or the future.'

'So they might be OK?'

'Might be. Always give people the benefit of the doubt. Even giant insect people with big mandibles and sharp pincer-claws, that's what I always say.'

'Right,' he went on, 'let's see if we can access what's left of the systems here and copy out the data.'

'Don't we need to analyse it and find out what it all means, what happened here?'

The Doctor sat down at the main console. He flexed his fingers over the keyboard. 'No. We can copy it into the TARDIS systems, let her do all the hard work.' He pressed a key and the main screen hummed into life.

'Good start,' Gisella said.

The Doctor was looking at the screen. 'But this is where it gets a bit more tricky.'

Activity

2 3 5 7 9 11 13 17 19 23

Red   Green   Yellow   Blue

1 2 4 8 16 32 46 64 128

Orbit Station 3 — Data Storage System. Select one number, word, or symbol from each set to continue.

The Doctor and Gisella studied the screen for a while.

'I think I've worked out the numbers,' Gisella said. 'Look, two is the only even number in the first set. And one is the only odd number in the second set.'

'That's a bit easy, though, isn't it?' the Doctor told her. 'There's another number in each set which I think is the odd one out. A prime candidate in the first set, and I think I can make a primary choice of colour from the words too.'

'Well, the bottom line is easy,' Gisella said. She pointed to the last but one symbol. 'Look, that's a diamond, with four sides. The others are all triangles with just three.'

'Can't fault you on that,' the Doctor agreed. He reached out and touched the diamond. It changed colour, and flashed. Then a big tick appeared at the end of the row of shapes. 'Gotcha,' the Doctor said happily.

'And you said you had a primary choice for the colours,' Gisella said. She reached over the Doctor's shoulder and tapped on the word *Green*. Another tick appeared. 'The only one that isn't a primary colour – it's made from blue and yellow.'

'Which just leaves us the numbers,' the Doctor said. 'You could be right about the evens and odds. But I think…' He tapped a number on the first line, and was again rewarded with a tick. 'Nine is the only number there that isn't a prime number. The only number that can be divided by another number apart from one and itself.'

'Three times three is nine,' Gisella agreed. 'But what about the third set, the other line of numbers. They're all even apart from one.'

'That's because they keep doubling,' the Doctor explained. 'One plus one gives us the two. Double that is four, then eight, sixteen, and so on. The number that doesn't fit is forty-six.' He tapped it, and the last tick appeared. 'Double thirty-two and you should go straight to sixty-four.'

Once they were into the system, the Doctor soon found the data he needed. It was damaged, and there were missing sections in the sequences of co-ordinates, times and observation. But he believed the TARDIS could repair some bits and guess at others.

Within ten minutes, the Doctor had copied the data on to an optical sphere. It looked like the same material as a CD or DVD, but was the size and shape of a golfball. He put it in his jacket pocket.

'Time for a cuppa. I reckon we've earned it.'

Through the door into the main control room, Gisella could see Commander Sarla talking to the Dravidian, Hive Captain Mantis.

'Let's take the short cut, and not disturb them,' the Doctor said, opening the other door.

On the way to the canteen they passed a work group repairing cables and pipes behind the wall. A large metal plate had been removed and was propped up nearby. Another Dravidian was helping cut new sections of cable with its powerful mandibles.

'It looks like they really are helping,' Gisella said.

'It does, doesn't it?' the Doctor agreed.

They found the canteen and joined a short queue of people waiting to be served drinks and snacks.

'Right, let's see if they can manage a decent cup of tea,' the Doctor said. 'And an iced bun. I like iced buns.'

But Gisella was staring across the large canteen. There were people sitting at tables, drinking coffee and eating snacks from plastic containers. At the back of the room, sitting at a table on their own, were two Dravidians. They were eating what looked like gooey orange spaghetti.

The Doctor saw where Gisella was looking. 'Even Dravidians have to eat,' he said.

'But didn't Commander Sarla say there were only three of them? Captain Mantis and two crew.'

'That's right,' the Doctor agreed. Then he frowned as he realized what Gisella meant. 'But Mantis is in main control, and we passed another Dravidian back down the corridor. With these two, that makes four of them.'

'So, what else are they lying about?' Gisella said quietly.

Into the Hive

'Are you sure this is a good idea?' Gisella asked a few minutes later.

'All my ideas are good,' the Doctor told her, closing the TARDIS doors behind them. 'I only ever have *good* ideas.'

The docking area where they had first arrived was as deserted as when the TARDIS had landed. But even so, Gisella and the Doctor were both whispering as they crept from the TARDIS to the large airlock doors.

'What if there are Dravidians waiting for us in there?' Gisella asked quietly.

'Why should there be? There are only a few of them, even if Hive Captain Mantis lied about the exact numbers. We can sneak in, have a look round, and be back out again before they've finished their tea break. The TARDIS will take a couple of hours to analyse the data sphere, so what have we got to lose?'

Gisella wasn't convinced, but she said nothing.

The airlock doors hissed open, and they went through into the chamber beyond. The Doctor checked the controls and gauges.

'There's air in the Dravidian ship. Rich in oxygen, but that's fine.'

He operated the main release valve, and the outer doors opened. Behind them was the door into the Dravidian ship. There was a round window set into it, and the Doctor peered through. Gisella had to stand on tip-toe. She could see an empty airlock, and through a similar window could see into the ship behind. The lighting was low, and tinged pale green. But the place seemed deserted.

'Shall we?' the Doctor asked.

'Of course.'

'Just a quick look round,' the Doctor said. 'Then we'll be gone before they ever knew we were here.'

The ship's airlock opened into a corridor. 'What are we looking for?' Gisella asked.

'Clues!'

'Clues?'

'Clues. If we can find the main control room, then we can access the flight computers and find out where they're really coming from and going to. I'd like to be sure it was a coincidence they were so close by and willing to help,' the Doctor grinned. 'And, you know, maybe it was. In which case, enough said. We'll see what the TARDIS makes of the data and leave them all to it. No harm done.'

'And if not?'

The Doctor considered for a moment. 'Then we might have to get *involved*,' he admitted. 'Not much. Just a smidge. Just enough to sort things out.'

'So, where do we start?'

The Doctor looked round. 'Well, the place seems pretty deserted. How about I start this way, and you start that way, and we'll meet back here in half an hour?'

The whole ship was lit with the same pale green lighting. The walls and floors and ceilings were all made of metal. But everything else had an organic feel to it – as if it had been grown rather than made.

As she explored along the corridor, Gisella looked in each room she passed. One was full of what looked like creepers and roots, growing from the walls and the ceiling and hanging down to form what might be hammocks and harnesses. Perhaps it was a rest area.

Another room was a control centre. The main console was a gnarled structure like an old tree stump. The controls and switches seemed to grow out of it like fungus – like mushrooms and toadstools. The dials were covered with tinted glass or plastic that looked like amber, and inside they seemed to be full of fluid. Gisella couldn't make sense of any of the readings, and she hoped the Doctor was having better luck.

She had almost got to the point when she would need to turn back, when she reached an archway set into the wall of the corridor. It was far larger than any of the other doors she had seen. What looked like a vine was growing over the archway, framing it and making it look important.

Well, Gisella thought, if she was heading back then this would be a good place to stop. One last room. It was obviously important. She would take a quick look, then go and find the Doctor and tell him what she'd found. If he thought it was important he could come and see for himself.

There was a control to open the door, set into the 'vine'. It was like a dark, knobbly growth protruding by several centimetres. Gisella pushed it, and the doors slid smoothly open.

The light inside was even greener than in the corridor. Gisella's first impression was of size – an enormous chamber stretching out in front of her. She must be looking into the very heart of the large ship. This room must take up most of the mid-section of the hull.

The roof was so high she couldn't see it. There was a canopy of creepers and cables and wires stretching into the distance and up out of sight. Thin veils of green mesh hung like curtains in front of her, obscuring Gisella's view of the chamber. She could tell it was big – enormous. But she couldn't see much more than that.

And there was a noise. It was like the chittering sound that Hive Captain Mantis had made. But it was constant, in the background, so quiet she could only just make it out.

Nervously, Gisella made her way forward. She pushed past the first of the curtains. It was damp and clammy, and heavier than it looked. Behind it was another.

As she made her way through the layers of the strange, green material the chittering sound got louder. There were shapes, barely more than shadows that got firmer and darker the more veils she passed.

One of the shapes *moved*.

Gisella froze, not daring to take another step. There was definitely movement ahead of her. Shadows and shapes blurred as something made its way slowly across the chamber. To her side, Gisella caught a glimpse of more movement – so fast she wondered if she'd imagined it. Until it happened again.

Then she realized that there was movement all round her.

She couldn't stay where she was. And she'd come too far into the enormous room to go back now without finding out what was happening, what was inside. It looked like there were only a few more of the veil-like curtains left. Gently, carefully, quietly, Gisella moved the next layer of material and went through.

Ahead of her, silhouetted against the next of the sheets of green, was the unmistakable shape of a Dravidian. Its spindly legs were moving rapidly, pincer-like claws snapping together. Its insect head moved slowly to and fro. Then, suddenly, it gave out a rapid burst of the chittering sound, and turned towards Gisella.

She was about to step back, hoping it wouldn't see her. But then Gisella decided she would be better staying absolutely still. The main light source was ahead of her, that was why the Dravidian was silhouetted so clearly. As it looked towards Gisella, it would be staring into darkness. She hoped.

For what seemed like an age, the creature just stood, staring at where Gisella was hiding. Had it seen her, or heard her? Was it watching and listening and waiting?

A second Dravidian loomed next to the first, another dark shadow in front of Gisella.

The chittering started again, getting more urgent and more rapid before the two creatures abruptly turned and moved off.

Relieved but shaken, Gisella gently pushed the last of the curtains aside and stared out into the heart of the chamber. Although she knew the two Dravidians couldn't be far away, although she could hear more of them deeper in the chamber, Gisella almost cried out in surprise at what she saw.

A massive cone took up the centre of the huge chamber. It reached up higher than Gisella could see. The cone was like an enormous honeycomb, made up of small hexagonal cells or compartments, each covered by a thin membrane.

The whole cone glowed with an eerie green light, and Gisella could see dark shapes within the cells. They were doubled over, curled into sleeping positions, but they were unmistakably Dravidians – one in each of the cells.

There were more compartments than Gisella could count. And she knew that the whole interior of the cone must be constructed in the same way – a maze of cells linked together. Each with a sleeping Dravidian inside. Thousands of them, waiting to hatch.

Knowing that she had to warn the Doctor, Gisella let the thin clammy curtain fall silently back into place. There were certainly more than just a few crew on board the ship. Despite what Mantis had told Commander Sarla, there was an entire hive of Dravidians. And Gisella guessed that whatever they were planning was not good for the crew of Orbit Station 3. She had to find the Doctor, and quickly.

Gisella made her way as quickly and quietly as she could back towards the door. She couldn't hear the chittering sound the Dravidians made any more, so perhaps they had gone.

Or perhaps, she suddenly thought, they had some reason for keeping quiet. But they couldn't know she was here – could they?

She thought there were just two more of the veils to get through, then she'd be back at the door. She gently eased the first aside, relieved to see only the final veil hanging behind it, moving gently as if in a breeze.

Gisella reached out for the last sheet of the thin, clammy substance. But before her hand reached it, the curtain was torn down. Shreds of material whipped past Gisella's face as it was ripped to pieces.

A Dravidian loomed over her. Viscous saliva dripped from its sharp mandibles as it gave an excited chitter. Its pincers shot out, reaching for Gisella.

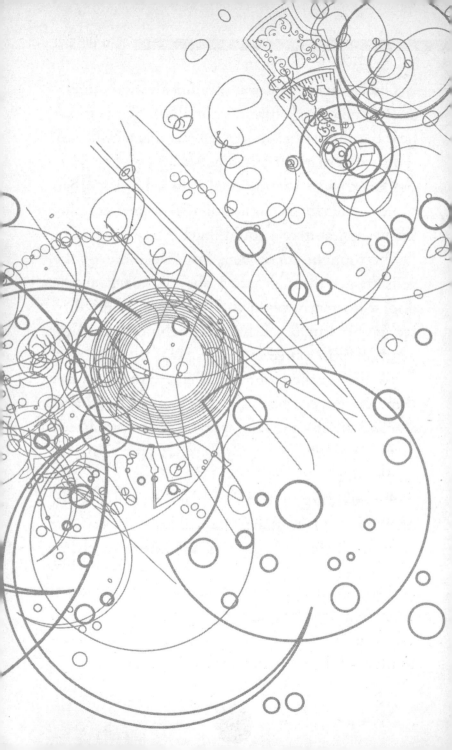

Unheeded Warnings

With a scream of surprise and fear, Gisella ran. She pushed through the damp curtains of material, thrust aside creepers and roots that hung down from the high roof. In seconds, she had no idea where she was any more. But she kept going. There must be more than one way out of the chamber, surely?

Through more of the clammy veils. She could hear the loud chittering close behind her. Was the Dravidian calling to others to help catch her? What would they do when they caught her?

Gisella barged through another of the curtains, and found herself staring at the back of a Dravidian. It started to turn, and she rushed past it and onwards. The chittering sound was getting louder as more of the creatures joined the search.

They were getting closer all the time. Gisella glanced over her shoulder, and saw the dark shapes pressing against the material behind her. The veil starting to move, pincers slicing down. She turned back and pushed through the next curtain, tangling for a moment in the thin, damp material and thrashing to get free. Then running again.

She turned, heading off in another direction, hoping the Dravidians would keep going.

But she slammed straight into something solid and unyielding. Something tall and thin that reached down towards her…

Gisella hit out, thumping at the creature holding her tight.

It gave a startled cry and let go. Gisella turned to run.

'You're stronger than you look, you know,' the Doctor said. He was doubled up from where Gisella had hit him. He held up his hand. 'Pax?'

'Sorry,' she gasped. 'Pax?'

'It means *peace*. OK – peace?'

'Peace,' Gisella agreed. 'But we have to get out of here.'

Behind them, one of the hanging curtains twitched, then started to move aside. Spindly claws reached round it.

But Gisella saw no more, because the Doctor grabbed her hand and together they ran as fast as they could.

'Doctor, the door's back that way,' Gisella gasped.

'Not the one *I* came through,' he told her.

They pushed through more of the dank fabric and Gisella saw that in front of them there was indeed another door. It wasn't as big or grand as the one she'd used.

The Doctor had his sonic screwdriver out as they ran. He held it in front of him like a talisman. The end glowed blue, and the door clicked open. The Doctor let Gisella go through ahead of him, then slammed the door shut.

The sonic screwdriver whirred again. There was a shower of sparks from the gnarled opening mechanism. From the other side of the door came the sound of something hammering against it and an angry chittering…

They didn't wait to see what would happen next. The Doctor led the way quickly back along the corridor to the main airlock where they had come in.

But the simple control panel with its single

control had gone. It was as if another whole panel had grown over the original one. Protruding from the panel was a set of controls.

'Lock down,' the Doctor said, examining it. 'Looks like they've activated some security system to stop us escaping.'

'Not very friendly,' Gisella said. She glanced down the corridor, expecting to see a group of angry Dravidians heading their way. But for the moment the corridor was clear.

'I need to work out the sequence,' the Doctor said. 'It must be a logical sequence or the Dravidians couldn't work it out.'

'Maybe they just know it?'

The Doctor shook his head. 'No, this was grown in response to a simple locking signal. Until it's actually here, they don't know what it will look like. The living matrix is programmed to create something that a Dravidian mind can understand.'

'Sonic screwdriver?' Gisella suggested.

'Could do. But the energy impulse might set fire to the whole panel, then we'd be trapped here.'

'So we have to work out the sequence,' Gisella realized. 'And before the Dravidians find us.'

Activity

Press the symbols in the right order
to open the main airlock door.

As soon as the airlock door was open, Gisella and the Doctor tumbled through.

'Lucky it wasn't any more complicated,' the Doctor said. 'I spotted the correct sequence at once.'

'Actually, it was me that pressed the symbols in the right order,' Gisella pointed out with a smile.

The Doctor didn't seem to hear her. 'Oh yes, logic is my strong point. One of my strong points. And I use the word "point" deliberately.'

Gisella nodded. 'First in the sequence – a circle, a single point. Then a line between two points.'

'That's what I was saying,' the Doctor said. 'Then a triangle joins three points, a square – that's four points. And then pentagram followed by hexagon. Easy.'

The Doctor had the outer door open now, and soon they were back on Orbit Station 3.

'We could just get in the TARDIS and see if it's finished analysing that data,' Gisella said. She pointed to the reassuring shape of the blue TARDIS in the corner of the airlock area.

'We could,' the Doctor agreed. 'But I think we should warn Commander Sarla that things aren't quite what they seem where the Dravidians are concerned, don't you?'

Gisella nodded. 'Yes,' she agreed. 'We should.'

They hurried to the main control room and found Commander Sarla talking with Lieutenant Jagellan. On the other side of the room, Captain Mantis was overseeing repair work on a control panel.

'What is it, Doctor?' the Commander asked as he saw the Doctor's grim expression.

'The Dravidians,' the Doctor said quietly, glancing at Mantis.

'What about them?'

'There's more than three of them, for one thing,' Gisella said. 'Their ship's got this enormous honeycomb full of them.'

'A hive,' the Doctor explained. 'About ready for hatching, I'd say. I'm sorry, but the Dravidians have been deceiving you. There are considerably more than three of them.'

Jagellan and Sarla looked at each other confused. Then Commander Sarla called Captain Mantis across to join them.

'I think there's been a bit of a misunderstanding,' the Commander said.

'Wopping great big one,' the Doctor corrected him. But Sarla ignored the Doctor. Mantis was rubbing his pincer-tipped forelegs together and chittering nervously.

'A misunderstanding? I do hope we have not misled you.' For a moment, the creature's segmented eyes stared right at Gisella. She could almost feel the Dravidian's hatred.

'The Doctor tells me there are more than three of you,' Sarala said. Then, surprisingly, he smiled.

Lietenant Jagellan gave a short laugh. 'Sorry, Doctor,' she said. 'And you, Gisella. But we know there are more than three of them.'

'But you said...' the Doctor started, confused.

'I said that Hive Captain Mantis and two of his crew were helping,' the Commander explained. 'But he is a *Hive* Captain. There's a clue in his title. We've always known that there's a full Dravidian hive on board that ship. It's a Hive Ship, after all.'

'I have a large crew,' Mantis said. He sounded almost apologetic. 'But most are busy maintaining the Hive. I could only allow two crew members to work on the station full time. A few more when they can be spared.' His head angled as he stared down at the Doctor and Gisella. 'Forgive me if you misunderstood.'

'But his crew tried to kill us,' Gisella said.

'On the Hive Ship?' Comander Sarla said.

'Well, yes.'

'We just popped over to say hello,' the Doctor said. 'See how things were going, that sort of thing.'

'You mean you were snooping around,' Lieutenant Jagellan said.

The Doctor sighed. 'Well, that too,' he admitted. 'But even so…'

'My crew was protecting the Hive,' Mantis said calmly. 'They were not to know you were just snooping. They felt the Hive was in danger and they acted to protect it.'

'Just a measured response, then?' the Doctor asked.

'Were you injured?' Mantis countered. 'Were you hurt at all?'

'No,' Gisella admitted. 'Just… frightened.'

'For that I apologize. But I feel you have only yourselves to blame. Perhaps next time you wish to look round my ship, you will ask permission. I shall be happy to show you whatever you want to see.'

'I'm sorry,' the Doctor said quickly. 'I can see that we've done you an injustice. We apologize. Don't we, Gisella,' he added, turning to her and winking.

'Oh yes,' she said. 'Sorry.'

'No harm done, then,' Commander Sarla said.

'None at all,' the Doctor said. 'I'll let Captain Mantis get back to…' He whipped out his glasses and popped them on, staring at the panel across the room where Mantis had been working. 'Oh look, still working on life support, I see. How very helpful.'

Commander Sarla and Lieutenant Jagellan were soon deep in their discussions again. The Doctor and Gisella left them to it.

'I guess we should be on our way then,' Gisella said.

'Oh, I don't know,' the Doctor said. 'Can't say I'm convinced.'

In the corridor outside, another Dravidian was waiting for them. It reared up, clicking its pincers and chittering excitedly.

'I have a message from Hive Captain Mantis,' it said quietly, looking round to check it could not be overheard.

'That's nice,' the Doctor said. 'And what's he want you to tell us that he couldn't say himself just now with the Commander listening? As if I didn't know.'

The creature stared down at them. 'Hive Captain Mantis says that if you try to interfere with our plans for this Orbit Station, you will be killed and fed to our younglings.'

Brief Briefing

The Doctor and Gisella watched the Dravidian scuttle away.

'Well, that's told us,' the Doctor said. 'And there was me, just thinking maybe we were wrong and should give them the benefit of the doubt.'

'Really?'

The Doctor shook his head. 'No, not really. The question is, what do we do about it?'

'The other question is, what are they up to? What do they think we can interfere with?' Gisella said. 'I mean, it's not like we're going to stop them repairing the life support and air systems, is it?'

'True,' the Doctor said thoughtfully. 'But unless we can persuade Commander Sarla that there's a problem, we're going to be a bit stuck for options anyway.' He sniffed. 'I say stuck, but maybe just constrained. Well, limited. Well…'

His voice tailed off as Lieutenant Jagellan walked up to them.

'Commander Sarla wonders if you could spare him a few minutes, in his briefing room,' she said.

'Perhaps this is our chance to convince him,' Gisella said.

'Brief briefing in the briefing room,' the Doctor mused. 'Could be. So, which way?' he asked Lieutenant Jagellan.

Commander Sarla was already waiting for them in the briefing room, which was close to the main control room. He stood up as the Doctor and Gisella entered and gestured for them to sit down at the big conference table that dominated the room. Lieutenant Jagellan sat the other side of the table, beside her Commander.

'You have to listen to us, Commander,' Gisella said at once.

The Comander raised his hand to stop her. 'In a minute. First let me show you something, and then we can move on to the things you want to discuss.'

'Like the fact the Dravidians are playing you for a fool, you mean?' the Doctor asked.

Gisella was surprised that this didn't seem to anger Commander Sarla. 'We lost all non-essential systems in the attack,' he said. 'The blast wave from the destruction of the other Orbit Stations severely damaged this Station and we're only just beginning to get things working again.'

'We know that,' the Doctor said impatiently. 'If you're going to tell us to stop causing trouble and let you get on with it, then just do it and we can move on to the more important matters.'

The Commander had a small remote control device in his hand, and operated it. An image appeared in the air, hanging impossibly above the table. It was a view along the corridor outside the main control room.

Lieutenant Jagellan said: 'One of the systems we've just got working again is the security network. Most of the cameras still need fixing, but this one is fine.'

Gisella watched as the Doctor and then herself walked into the image.

'You were spying on us,' she accused.

'I was,' Commander Sarla admitted. 'I did think you were out to cause trouble.'

'We're really not,' the Doctor assured him.

'Why would you be so adamant that the Dravidians are not as helpful as they seem, that they are a threat, I wondered? So I ordered the parts of the security net that are working again to follow and monitor you.'

A Dravidian appeared in the image as the camera moved. It was waiting for the Doctor and Gisella.

Commander Sarla tapped at the remote control. 'I'm afraid the microphones are still not working as well as they should,' he said.

But the Dravidian's words were clear enough for them all to hear: 'Hive Captain Mantis says that if you try to interfere with our plans for this Orbit Station, you will be killed and fed to our younglings.'

The image disappeared as Commander Sarla pressed another button on the remote and put it down on the table. 'Now,' he said, 'if I go to Mantis, he will no doubt tell me that the Dravidian was merely warning you not to interrupt their work helping us to repair the systems.'

'No doubt,' the Doctor said quietly.

'But that isn't what it meant at all,' Gisella told them.

Sarla nodded. 'I think you're right,' he admitted.

'And something else you said seems to ring true as well. Something I'm not sure I quite understand.'

'And what's that?' Gisella asked.

'About how the Dravidians seem focused on the life support systems,' Jagellan replied. 'Obviously they were a priority. But they're fixed now, yet Mantis and his crew are still working on them. They insist everything has to be perfect.'

'And it isn't?' the Doctor asked.

Commander Sarla took a deliberate, deep breath. 'Taste that,' he said.

The Doctor nodded. 'They haven't got the mix right yet, have they? Still too much oxygen. In fact, it's getting more extreme. Can't be that hard to get the mixture of air right, can it?'

'No,' Jagellan said. 'It can't.'

'So what are they up to?' Sarla asked.

'Doctor!' Gisella said as she remembered something. 'The Dravidian Hive Ship – that had an oxygen rich atmosphere, remember? Maybe they just don't know what the right mixture for humans should be.'

'Maybe,' the Doctor conceded. 'Or maybe there's something else going on here.'

'There is one other thing,' Jagellan said slowly.

'What's that?'

'The Dravidian Ship is hooked into our power systems. At first they were helping us keep the Station going. But our own reactors are working fine now, and the Dravidians are drawing back power to recharge their fuel cells.'

'That sounds fair enough,' Gisella said.

'Except,' Jagellan told them, 'the amount of power they are taking is huge. Far more than they could possibly need to recharge their own systems, or even run their ship if they didn't have any power supply of their own.'

The Doctor turned to Commander Sarla. 'You're right to be suspicious, but to be sure we can stop them, we need to know what the Dravidians are planning.'

'And where can we find that out?' Sarla asked.

'On board their ship,' the Doctor said. 'Mantis warned us not to go back there, and he'll expect you to go along with his wishes. So it's the last place they'll expect us to look. And we need to know what they're doing with all that power.'

Jagellan and Sarla wanted to arm themselves with blasters. But the Doctor persuaded them that if they were armed, it would be harder to claim they were just innocently looking round the Hive Ship.

'If we're dead, though, we won't need an excuse,' Lieutenant Jagellan pointed out.

The Doctor shrugged. 'So, don't get dead. Trust me, I'm right about this. Look at me, I've been caught doing so many things I shouldn't so many times I've lost count, and I'm not dead.'

'You only need to be wrong once,' Jagellan pointed out.

Just as before, the Hive Ship seemed to be deserted. Repairs had grown over the damaged control panels. The Doctor led the way into the ship, along the outer corridor, and to the small door where he and Gisella had escaped from the Hive Chamber.

'Best to use the tradesman's entrance,' he told them. 'If we get caught, we'll bluff our way out. You can tell them you brought us back to apologize.'

'Like they'll believe that,' Gisella murmured.

But the Doctor was too busy opening the door to hear her. He put his finger to his lips to signal for them all to be quiet, and led the way through.

Gisella pushed through the dank curtains of flimsy green material again. The light was brighter than she remembered, but perhaps they were just nearer the huge cone of the Hive.

Behind her, Sarla and Jagellan could not hide their distaste as they too fought their way through the clammy material.

After what seemed a very long time, the Doctor stopped. He waited for the others to reach him, then whispered: 'Just one more sheet of this stuff to go, then you'll see the Hive. Hopefully we can find some control systems linked into it that will explain what's going on and what their plan for your Orbit Station might be.'

The light was definitely brighter than it had been before. Gisella mentioned it to the Doctor, and he told them that perhaps it was just because the ship had more power now and the lighting was turned up.

But when they pushed through the last veil of the green material, they saw at once that it wasn't the case.

The light was coming from the vast honeycomb of the Hive. It had been glowing a pale green before. Now it was brilliant yellow. Gisella could feel the heat coming off it. She could see the silhouettes of the Dravidians within their honeycombed cells.

And she could see that slowly, hesitantly, uncertainly at first, they were coming to life. Feelers and mandibles moved, heads swung slowly back and forth. Legs stretched. Forelegs scythed through the thin sheeting over the front of one of the cells as the Dravidian inside forced its way out.

The Hatching Horror

The entire massive Hive was coming to life. All round the enormous cone, Dravidians were forcing their way out of the cells and climbing down to gather in the chamber. As each Dravidian emerged from its cells, others pushed through from behind, where they had been sleeping deep within the Hive.

'There are thousands of them!' Commander Sarla said.

'A mass hatching,' the Doctor said grimly. 'They needed the power from your reactors to warm things up and accelerate the growth cycle of their younglings.'

'And now they're all waking up and coming out,' Gisella said.

'Like an army,' Jagellan added.

'Not just *like* an army,' the Doctor told them. 'This *is* an army. An army of Dravidians that I would guess is about to invade your Orbit Station.'

'But why?' the Commander asked. 'It's just an Orbit Station, and one that's recently been attacked and almost destroyed.'

'I think we might be about to find out,' Gisella said. 'Look – isn't that Captain Mantis?'

Across the huge chamber, a Dravidian was emerging from the veils of green material hanging from the roof. It was slightly larger than the others, slightly darker. It moved with an authority and confidence the other Dravidians lacked. Several more of the creatures were close behind it, bowing their heads and chittering noisily. It was, they could all now see, definitely Hive Captain Mantis.

Mantis stopped in front of the gathering crowd of Dravidians from the Hive. The chittering they were all making gradually died down.

'If he's going to make a speech,' the Doctor said, 'then I hope he knows some good jokes.' His eyes brightened. 'Actually, I heard this one the other century about a Venusian Shanghorn who was given a Perigosto stick, and what happened was that…'

'Shhh,' Gisella hissed at him. 'Mantis has started speaking.'

'Oh,' the Doctor said. 'Right. Sorry. Maybe he knows that one.'

'My children!' Hive Captain Mantis announced. 'I welcome you as you rise from your sleep and leave the Hive for the first time. I welcome you to the Great Hive Ship, and to your destiny.'

'What's he on about?' Jagellan whispered.

The Doctor shrugged.

'We are at this moment on the brink of a great discovery. A wonderful secret. Knowledge that could put the Dravidians among the most feared and powerful races in the galaxy!'

'Don't like the sound of that,' the Doctor said to his friends.

'What are they after?' Commander Sarla wondered. 'What do they think we have that could be so useful to them?'

'The Orbit Station to which we are docked holds a terrible secret,' Mantis was saying. 'The pathetic humans who live here do not even realize they have such power in their hands. They have been attacked, and they are happy to survive. That is all – just to survive.'

'Sounds good enough to me,' Jagellan said.

'We observed the attack,' Mantis said. 'From a safe distance, many parsecs away, we watched the energy trace that burned across these heavens. But we were too distant to record any useful data or to analyse the weapon that was used so that we might build our own to the same design.'

'So that's it,' the Doctor murmured.

'They want to copy the weapon,' Gisella realized.

'The humans are so weak,' Mantis went on, 'they do not realize that the data their Orbit Station recorded when it survived the attack would tell them how to adapt their own x-ray lasers to make them just as powerful against any enemy they chose to fight. But they are too weak and stupid to see it. So we shall crush them and take the data we need.'

There was an enthusiastic chittering from the thousands of Dravidians now packed into the chamber. Still more of the creatures were climbing down from the Hive. The crowd was spreading – the nearest Dravidians getting very close to where the Doctor, Gisella, Sarla and Jagellan were now hiding behind a single, flimsy sheet of green.

'And when we have the information we need,'

Mantis proclaimed, 'then we shall wipe it from their data banks. We shall destroy all evidence of the weapon – destroy this Orbit Station and all the humans on it, so that our secret will remain safe and hidden until we choose to make use of it.'

'You were right about this not sounding good,' Commander Sarla whispered to the Doctor.

The Doctor nodded. 'Time we were going, I think. I'll see if I can lock the doors and keep them in here for a bit while we work out a plan.'

'There are thousands of them,' Lieutenant Jagellan said. 'It'll have to be some plan!'

'Don't worry,' Gisella told her as they made their way quietly and carefully back towards the door. 'The Doctor's good at plans.'

'First part of the plan is to get back to main control on the Orbit Station,' the Doctor said. 'And the second part is to destroy the data they're looking for. If it doesn't exist, maybe we can persuade them to go away and leave us alone.'

'Or not,' Jagellan said.

The Doctor nodded. 'Or, as you say, not.'

'But isn't that exactly the data you were after, Doctor?' Sarla asked.

'Don't worry,' Gisella told him, 'we've got a copy.'

'And we're not planning on making our own weapon from it,' the Doctor added.

Ahead of him, Jagellan skidded to a halt. 'Pity,' she said. 'Because it might be useful.'

In front of her was a Darvidian. It reared up high on its hind legs, pincers snipping the air as it regarded them through its segmented eyes.

Without thinking, Gisella ran straight for the Dravidian. She bent down low, thumping her shoulder into the creature's legs. A pincer grazed past her ear. Another snapped shut close to her arm.

But the Dravidian was falling, its legs knocked away from under it.

'Well done, Gisella,' the Doctor called as he helped her back to her feet. 'The advantage of being knee-high to a giant grasshopper!'

They raced after Sarla and Jagellan to the outer door, and through into the corridor.

'Change of plan,' the Doctor said. 'No time to lock them in now they know we're here. We have to get back to main control and warn the people on the Orbit Station. And fast!'

They ran through the corridors of Orbit Station 3. Anyone they saw, Commander Sarla and Lieutenant Jagellan shouted warnings to. They told them to get to the main control room and the surrounding area.

'We can barricade ourselves in the control area,' Sarla explained. 'While you sort out this great plan of yours.'

'Working on it,' the Doctor confirmed. 'Getting there.'

'What are you thinking?' Gisella asked.

'I'm thinking it's a bit odd that Hive Captain Mantis has waited all this time before making his move. Why not take over the Station as soon as the Dravidians arrived? The crew would have been much less able to defend themselves.'

They raced into the main control room. Commander Sarla was already shouting orders. Pictures from the security cameras in the main docking area appeared above the main control console.

A siren sounded, and an announcement that everyone should: 'Go immediately to your safe areas at main control. This is not a drill,' the voice explained.

Gisella recognized Chief Engineer Tyrall working at one of the other consoles. The bright lights glistened on his bald, sweaty head. 'Got something here, sir,' he called.

'What is it?' Sarla asked.

'Looks like another ship approaching. They're a long way out, though. Won't get here for a while so I don't think they'll be much help. Whoever they are,' he added, checking some of the controls. 'I don't recognize that type at all.'

'Do you, Doctor?' Gisella asked.

He nodded. He didn't look happy. 'I do, and you're right – they won't help. We need to sort out the Dravidians, and fast.'

'Why?' Gisella asked quietly. 'Who is it?'

'Dreadbringers,' the Doctor replied. 'Looks like the Darksmiths have tracked us down again.'

But there was no time to discuss it. The image of the docking area still floated above the control console. As everyone watched, the main airlock burst open. A horde of Dravidians rushed through into the Orbit Station. The main control room was filled with the distorted sound of thousands of Dravidians chittering with relish as they hurried to attack their human enemies.

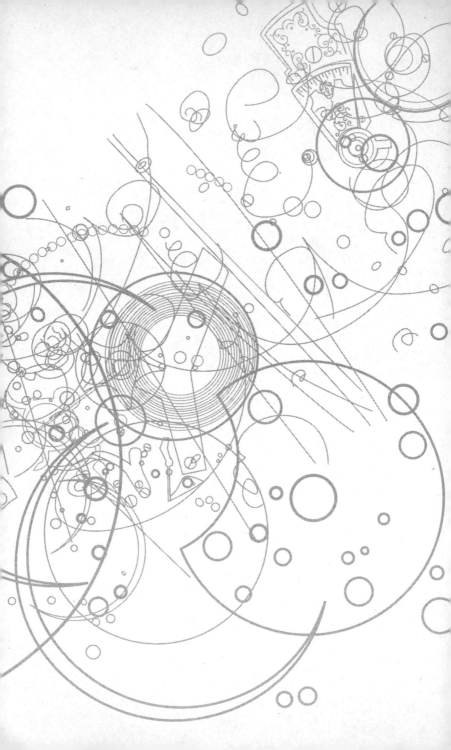

The Taking of Orbit Station 3

'Seal the area!' ordered Commander Sarla.

Thick metal shutters slowly came down all round the control room. Similar shutters were descending over doorways throughout the area, offering protection – at least for a while – to the Orbit Station crew members behind them.

On the floating screen, Gisella could see the Dravidians rampaging through the Orbit Station. They rushed like a tidal wave along corridors, swarmed into rooms, tore metal plates from the walls and control consoles from the floor. They seemed determined to cause as much damage as possible as they headed towards the main control areas.

The Doctor was walking in a circle round the image that hung in the air. Round and round he went, tapping his chin, putting on his glasses then taking them off again. He paused, mouth open in sudden realization. Then he sighed and shook his head and let out a dismissive 'No,' before carrying on round the image.

'Yes!' the Doctor suddenly decided. 'Oh yes. Life support. Air filtration. Oxygen system. Giant insects!'

'He gets like this,' Gisella said to Commander Sarla.

'So I gathered.'

The Doctor ran over to them. 'That's it, don't you see?'

Sarla looked at Gisella, who turned to Lieutenant Jagellan. She looked back at Sarla.

'Actually, Doctor,' the Commander said, 'I don't think we do.'

'They're insects, right?'

'Looks that way,' Jagellan agreed.

'But you don't get insects that big. Not on most Earth-type planets. Why not?' He clicked his fingers and pointed at Gisella. 'Come on, come on – why not?!'

'Well, because you just don't.'

'But you used to,' the Doctor insisted. 'In prehistoric times, giant insects. Well, maybe not giant but bigger than your average insect. Much bigger.'

'Does this help?' Sarla asked.

'Oh yes,' the Doctor told him. 'Because I'll tell you why you don't get giant insects. Oxygen!'

'Oxygen?' Jagellan shook her head. 'You've lost me.'

'Insects don't have lungs. They don't draw in the air like we do. They breathe through tiny holes call spiracles in their sides. The air just wafts in and they strip it of the oxygen they need. But it's a very inefficient system, and it won't support insect life bigger than about this.' He demonstrated with his thumb and forefinger, estimating the size of a typical insect.

'Are you saying the Dravidians shouldn't exist?' Gisella asked. 'Or that they're not insects?'

'No, no, no,' the Doctor insisted. 'In prehistoric times, you got bigger insects because the air was richer in oxygen. They could get more oxygen more quickly and that supported bigger bodies.'

He turned and pointed at the images of the Dravidians rampaging through the Orbit Station. 'To be that big and that active, they need loads of oxygen. Tonnes of it. All the time. That's why the air in their ship is so oxygen-rich. And that's why they didn't hatch out and attack earlier.'

Commander Sarla was nodding. 'When Mantis and his crew first got here they were very sluggish and tired. They said it was because the life support wasn't working properly.'

'And they fixed it, to make the air in the Station rich enough in oxygen for them,' Jagellan realized.

'And now that they're pumping out such a high proportion of oxygen they can attack.'

'So what do we do?' Gisella asked.

'Whatever it is,' Jagellan told them, 'it will have to be quick.' She pointed at the images of swarming Dravidians. 'They're right outside!'

Almost as soon as she finished speaking, the shutters rattled and shook. There was a heavy clang as something slammed into the other side of them. Soon the noise was like thunder, and dents were appearing in the metal.

'They're trying to get in,' Gisella said. 'How long have we got?'

'Long enough,' the Doctor decided. 'If I can change the life support systems so the air that's circulated round the Station has less oxygen in it, that'll force the Dravidians to retreat to their ship or collapse.'

'What about us, Doctor?' Jagellan asked. 'Don't we need oxygen too?'

'Not as much. I can set it to a level where the humans feel a bit tired and breathless but the Dravidians who don't leave will collapse.'

'Then let's get started.' Commander Sarla had to shout to be heard above the battering at the shutters.

One of the shutters was already bending out of shape. A thin Dravidian arm forced its way through, pincers snapping.

'Chief Engineer Tyrall!' Sarla yelled. 'Get over here and give the Doctor all the help he needs.'

'What's the plan, Doctor?' Tyrall wanted to know.

The Doctor quickly explained about changing the mixture of the air so there was less oxygen. As they spoke, a Dravidian was forcing its way round the edge of the bent shutter. It was Hive Captain Mantis.

Several of the Orbit Station Crew ran to fight Mantis off – beating at the Dravidian Captain with chairs and spanners and clipboards, and anything else that came to hand.

'Should be easy enough, Doctor,' Tyrall said.

He led the way over to a control panel at the back of the room. On it was a dial and three small control knobs. They were labelled A, B and C, and each had a pointer on it that related to a scale round the edge.

'It's easy enough,' Tyssan said. 'You change the mix of oxygen, nitrogen and other gases here. A is the oxygen, B the nitrogen, and C is a mix of other gases like argon and carbon dioxide.'

The Doctor reached for the A knob and was about to adjust it when Gisella stopped him.

'Wait,' she said. 'Weren't the Dravidians working on this? How do we know they haven't sabotaged it or something.'

'Good point,' the Doctor agreed. He used his sonic screwdriver to remove the whole front panel of the console. Inside was a maze of twisting pipes and cables. 'I don't think it ought to look like that,' the Doctor said.

Tyrall shook his head. 'They've rerouted everything. We only have time to try one combination of gases, if we get it wrong we're dead. But we'll never work out which control is linked to the oxygen now.'

Activity

Work out which control operates the Oxygen and turn it down. Turn up Nitrogen and Other Gases to compensate.

A B C

Nitrogen Control   Other Gases Control   Oxygen Control

Slowly but surely the blast shutters were being twisted and broken. The sheer weight of the Dravidians outside was breaking through. A second of the creatures squeezed through a gap after its Captain and joined the fight.

Then a third was inside, pincers snapping, mandibles dripping viscous saliva.

'We're out of time,' Lieutenant Jagellan said. 'Even if you get the right control for the oxygen now, it will take a minute for it to start to have an effect.'

'She's right,' Commander Sarla said. 'It was a brave attempt Doctor. A good plan. But we've lost.'

Air of Victory

'**W**e haven't lost yet,' Gisella cried. She ran towards the attacking Dravidians.

Commander Sarla tried to grab her as she passed, but the Doctor stopped him.

'You can't let a little girl risk her life like that,' Lieutenant Jagellan protested.

'She's stronger than she looks,' the Doctor told them all. 'And she's not really a little girl.' But he didn't explain any more than that.

'What's she doing?' Chief Engineer Tyrall asked.

Gisella had not run to the assistance of the crew members who were fighting off the three Dravidians. Nor was she helping the other crew who were struggling to keep more Dravidians from forcing their way inside. She ran to the side of the room where there was a first aid kit on the wall.

'Like that'll help,' Jagellan said.

But it wasn't the first aid kit that Gisella was after. Underneath it, in a rack attached to the foot of the wall, were three fire extinguishers. After a quick examination, Gisella grabbed one that had a long cone-like nozzle attached rather than a hosepipe.

'Of course,' the Doctor said. 'You clever little girl!'

'I thought you said she wasn't a little girl,' the Commander told him.

'I'm right about the clever though. Watch!'

Gisella aimed the fire extinguisher at the nearest Dravidian – Hive Captain Mantis. A burst of what looked like steam erupted from the nozzle, spraying over the Dravidian. But it wasn't steam, it was carbon dioxide.

Starved of oxygen, Captain Mantis weakened. Another spraying, and he collapsed to his knees, then keeled over. Gisella hurried to train the extinguisher on the next Dravidian.

But the two remaining creatures had seen what was happening and backed away towards the straining shutters.

'You'd better take your Hive Captain with you,' the Doctor called after them.

Gisella backed off enough to allow them to help

Mantis to his feet. The creature turned to look at the Doctor. Its eyes were full of anger and hatred. But as other crew members armed themselves with fire extinguishers he dared not attack.

'You cannot hold out in here for ever,' Mantis warned them. 'Those puny weapons won't last for long, and then what will you do?'

'Already done it,' the Doctor told him proudly. 'I've changed the mix of the air supply, despite your tinkering.' He took a deep breath. 'Oh yes – control B is linked to the oxygen now. C is the nitrogen and A the mix of other gases. It'll take a few minutes but already the oxygen levels are falling.'

'You need oxygen too,' Mantis said.

'Not as much as you do. And I'm sure Commander Sarla and his crew will be happy to take things easy for a while if it means they're rid of you.' His voice changed – becoming more serious and threatening. 'Go back to your ship. Leave this Orbit Station and never come back. Never come anywhere near Ursolonamex ever again. If you do, we'll be waiting.'

Mantis stared back at the Doctor. For a moment it looked like he was about to reply. But then he staggered weakly to the shutters and followed the other two Dravidians back through.

'You have not seen the last of us, Doctor!' Mantis shouted back through the shutter.

'Oh yes I have,' the Doctor told him. 'No more warnings, no second chances. Now – get lost!'

The floating image from the security cameras showed the Dravidians hurrying back towards their ship.

'Are they really going?' Jagellan asked.

'Oh yes,' the Doctor told her.

As he finished speaking, the Orbit Station echoed with a loud clang. The ground shifted slightly under their feet.

'What was that?' Gisella asked, setting down the fire extinguisher.

'Company,' the Doctor said grimly.

'More Dravidians?' Commander Sarla wondered. 'They won't dare come in with the oxygen levels so low.' He took a deep breath and sat down on the floor. 'Makes things a bit tiring though,' he admitted.

'It's not more Dravidians,' the Doctor said. Everyone else was taking deep breaths and leaning against walls or sitting on the floor now. Only the Doctor and Gisella seemed unaffected.

'Then – who?' Tyrall asked.

'Just ignore them,' the Doctor said. 'They'll soon discover that what they're after isn't here any more and leave you in peace. Then you can sort out the oxygen levels and get back to repairing the Station.'

The image above the main control panel changed to show a secondary airlock. The unmistakeable shape of a Dreadbringer was climbing through into the Station. Soon there were a dozen of the Darksmiths' military elite. They marched through the Orbit Station, apparently not caring about the lack of oxygen. They were looking for the Doctor and Gisella.

A group of retreating Dravidians saw the approaching Dreadbringers and hurried on their way, chittering in agitation. All across Orbit Station 3, the Dravidians hastened their escape. Soon their Hive Ship was undocking and heading rapidly away.

'Well done, Doctor!' Commander Sarla exclaimed. 'You did it. They've gone. But what are those?' he pointed at the image of the Dreadbringers now methodically searching the Station.

There was no answer.

When Commander Sarla, Lietenant Jagellan,

Engineer Tyrall and everyone else turned to look, they found that the Doctor and Gisella had gone.

'Was it worth it?' Gisella wondered.

'Not for this, I'm afraid,' the Doctor said.

They were back in the TARDIS, safe from the searching Dreadbringers. The TARDIS had finished analysing the surveillance data from Orbit Station 3's systems. But all it showed was a massive energy surge as the mysterious attackers had fired their weapons.

The Doctor tapped the TARDIS screen. 'There's a trail, an energy trace from their engines. So we know where one of the ships that was involved went after the attack on Ursolonamex.'

'But that's great,' Gisella told him. 'That means we can follow them.'

The Doctor nodded. 'True. But we didn't really need this data to find out where they're headed. But I'm glad we came. If we hadn't been here, the Dravidians wouldn't have discovered anything useful either, but they might still have destroyed the Orbit Station and killed Commander Sarla and everyone else.'

'You said we didn't need the data to know where

the attackers went,' Gisella said. 'Why's that? Do you know where they were going?'

'Could have guessed,' the Doctor said. 'The energy trail leads back to Karagula. The planet of the Darksmiths. So we still don't know who they are working for or how to destroy the Eternity Crystal.'

'Then we need a new plan,' Gisella told him. 'We can't just give up. However risky and dangerous it might be, we have to do something.'

The Doctor was busily setting the TARDIS controls. 'You're absolutely right,' he said. 'Nice trick with the fire extinguisher, by the way. Good thinking.'

'Thanks.'

'Right, all set.' The Doctor operated the control that opened the TARDIS doors. 'Just one more little thing for me to do, and then the TARDIS is off to Karagula.'

'Where are you going?' Gisella asked as the Doctor headed for the doors.

'Outside. Just for a minute. There's nothing to worry about. Just one last thing I need to do before we go.'

The Doctor stepped into the docking area, carefully

closing the TARDIS door behind him. He took a deep breath and nodded happily. Chief Engineer Tyrall had turned up the oxygen again. Soon Orbit Station 3 would be getting back to normal.

He turned back to the TARDIS.

And strong arms grabbed him as a Dreadbringer stepped out of the shadows. Its armoured helmet was so close to the Doctor's face he could see his reflection in the polished surface.

'At last we have you, Doctor,' the Dreadbringer rasped. 'You are our prisoner, and there can be no escape this time!'

To be continued...

TARDIS

Data Bank

The Dravidians

An insectoid race from the Dravidian Star Cluster of Ganeymede Antares, the Dravidians are ambitious for an empire. But so far their efforts to conquer other races have generally been thwarted. But they are constantly on the look out for technology and weapons that will help them defeat their enemies.

Like all insects, the Dravidians breathe through spiracles — small holes in their abdomen.

There are other similarities with the insect life of Earth. For example, the thin yellow blood of a Dravidian does not carry oxygen round the body.

The Dravidians need air that is very rich in oxygen to stay active and survive. The largest insect on Earth is the Goliath Beetle which lives in the tropics and can grow to about 15 centimetres long. But most Earth insects are less than 1 centimetre long, largely because of the amount of oxygen in Earth's atmosphere.

To find out what events lie in store
for the Doctor and the mystery of the
Darksmith Legacy, look out for
The Pictures of Emptiness.
But for now, here is a taste of
things to come....

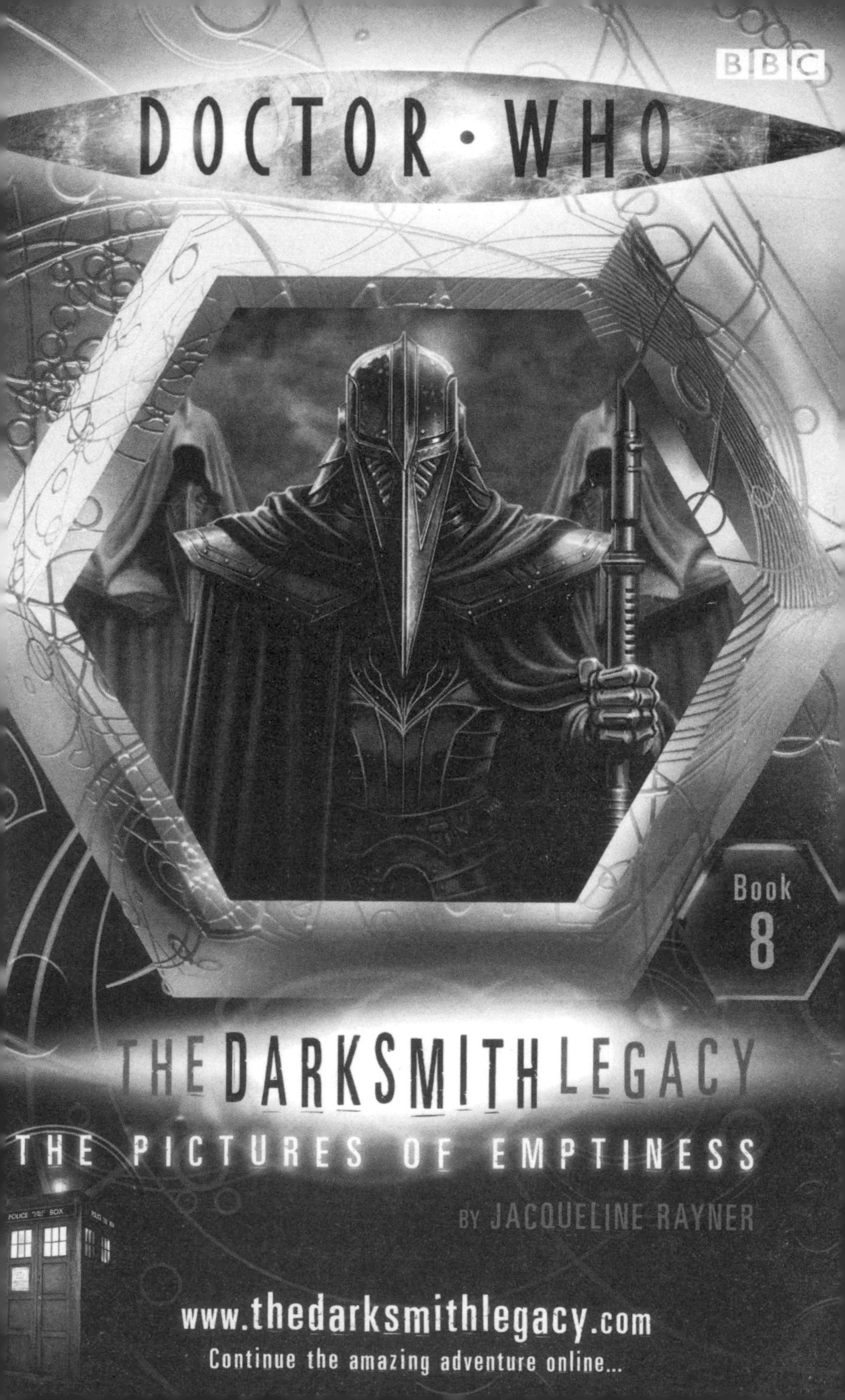
BBC
DOCTOR · WHO
Book 8
THE DARKSMITH LEGACY
THE PICTURES OF EMPTINESS
BY JACQUELINE RAYNER
www.thedarksmithlegacy.com
Continue the amazing adventure online...

Captured

Many hours later, the Doctor was led into a round room. Tiers of benches encircled a central dais, and rows of orange lights glowed from a domed ceiling. The Doctor felt like he was standing in a hollowed-out pumpkin. The rows of skeletal Darksmiths starring at him from the benches only reinforced the Hallowe'en impression; when the Adjudicator arrived the Doctor half expected him to say 'Trick or treat?'

He didn't, of course. He was a member of the Shadow Proclamation, and as such extremely dignified. And the Doctor was very pleased to see him.

He was the reason the Time Lord had allowed himself to be captured.

It wasn't that the Doctor really minded being on the run. It happened so often that he sometimes found it a bit boring if no one was chasing him. But when he had an important job on hand – like destroying the dangerously powerful Eternity Crystal – relentless pursuers could really get in the way. How much easier if they were called off.

The Shadow Proclamation were just the beings to do that.

The Doctor had realized that if the Darksmiths had now officially involved their Dreadbringers, then everything would have to be done properly – completely above board. In an affair this big, he had hoped that meant a representative of the Shadow Proclamation would be involved, and he was relieved to discover that he'd been right. OK, so he might not get away with much under the Adjudicator's stern eye – which didn't mean that he wouldn't try – but at least his trial would be fair.

And the Doctor being the Doctor, he might just have a trick or two up his sleeve...

Once on the dais, the Doctor's two glass-fleshed warders let go of him and retired to a front bench. He rubbed his forearms and looked around for a seat. Obligingly, a white shape began to form out of the floor behind him. He sank back into it as it moulded itself to his body, while at the other end of the dais, a similar structure was preparing itself for the Adjudicator. However, while the Adjudicator's chair kept growing up and up, allowing the judge to look down on the defendant and the surrounding Darksmiths, the Doctor's not only remained low, but also shaped itself around his limbs, creating white plasticky cuffs that gripped his forearms and calves.

'Hey!' he called out in surprise, as he found himself unable to move – but thought better of protesting too much. At least the moulded chair meant that he was comfortable, which certainly hadn't been the case for most of his courtroom appearances. Really, he did seem to be put on trial an awful lot for someone who was only ever trying to help...

'The defendant will give his name and designation,' boomed the Adjudicator.

'Certainly, your shadowy honour,' said the Doctor with a polite nod. 'I am known as the Doctor, the last of the Time Lords of Gallifrey.'

A murmur passed round the courtroom, spinning dizzily through the massed Darksmiths. Not all of them had known who – or rather, what – they were dealing with. The Doctor smiled slightly inside.

Any advantage...

The pale Adjudicator, however, coolly professional, gave no start of recognition, no gasp of horror. 'Relate the charge, High Minister Drakon,' he said, addressing a tall Darksmith, the only one who had a seat on the dais.

Drakon rose to his feet. 'The charge is theft of Darksmith property, namely the so-called Eternity Crystal,' he said.

'Not guilty!' called the Doctor.

Drakon glared. 'There can be no question of your guilt. The Crystal has been in your possession for the last three-hundred vectors!'

'Hey!' The Doctor turned to the Adjudicator. 'He's prejudicing the trial! I'm innocent until proven guilty, m'lud.'

The Adjudicator raised a hand, but said nothing. He seemed to be processing information. The Doctor, who had expected just to be told to be quiet, was slightly taken aback.

Finally the Adjudicator spoke. 'Innocent until proven guilty. A legal standard found on 87 member planets and 12932 affiliated worlds. This form of trial is acceptable under Article 1768C. The court will proceed in accordance with this directive.' He paused for a moment, blinked and resumed his previous expression, then he turned to Drakon. 'The trial will begin. State your evidence.'

But the Doctor's head was churning with new ideas. 'Ooh, wait wait wait,' he called, trying but failing to raise a hand to attract the judge's attention.

The Adjudicator looked at him. 'Yes?'

'Itchy nose,' said the Doctor. 'Could the court appoint someone to scratch it?'

The Adjudicator ignored him. 'The trial will begin,' he repeated pointedly.

'Ooh, wait wait wait,' the Doctor called again.

'The accused is wasting the court's time!' shouted Drakon.

'I most certainly am not,' replied the Doctor indignantly, having gained the few seconds he needed to process his thoughts. 'If anything, I'm saving it time. Do I understand correctly' – he turned to the Adjudicator – 'that under Article 1768C, any legitimate trial form may be used in a Shadow Proclamation hearing?'

'If appropriate and approved by a majority of recognized legal systems,' agreed the Adjudicator.

'Good,' said the Doctor. 'Then I demand to be tried by a jury of my peers.'

DOCTOR · WHO

THE DARKSMITH LEGACY

'Collected' Party

Celebrate the epic Darksmith Legacy experience with an out-of-this-world party to be held in a secret London location during the October half-term 2009, after the final exciting instalment has been published.

For your chance to win an exclusive ticket to this Doctor Who Extravaganza you must sign up at www.thedarksmithlegacy.com, complete the quest online and submit your details. We will let you know if you have been successful via email.

This will be a once in a lifetime opportunity to win lots of Doctor Who prizes and see scary monsters up-close...
...Don't miss out!

More party details will be revealed in another dimension on the Darksmith website so keep checking back for further updates. Full Terms and Conditions can also be found at www.thedarksmithlegacy.com.

DOCTOR·WHO

Fantastic free Doctor Who slipcase offer when you buy two Darksmith Legacy books!

Limited to the first 500 respondents!

To be eligible to receive your free slipcase, fill in your details on the form below and send along with original receipt(s) showing the purchase of two Darksmith Legacy books. The first 500 correctly completed forms will receive a slipcase.

Offer subject to availability. Terms and conditions apply. See overleaf for details.

ere ┄┄┄┄┄┄┄┄┄┄┄┄┄┄┄┄┄┄┄┄┄┄┄┄

Entry Form

Name: ....

Address: ....

Email: ....

Have you remembered to include your two original sales receipts? ⬡

I have read and agree to the terms and conditions overleaf. ⬡

Tick here if you don't want to receive marketing communications from Penguin Brands and Licensing. ⬡

Important – Are you over 13 years old?

If you are 13 or over just tick this box, you don't need to do anything else. ⬡

If you are under 13, you must get your parent or guardian to enter the promotion on your behalf. If they agree, please show them the notice below.

Notice to parent/guardian of entrants under 13 years old

If you are a parent/guardian of the entrant and you consent to the retention and use of the entrant's personal details by Penguin Brands and Licensing for the purposes of this promotion, please tick this box. ⬡

Name of parent/guardian: ....

Terms and Conditions

1. This promotion is subject to availability and is limited to the first 500 correctly completed respondents received.
2. This promotion is open to all residents aged 7 years or over in the UK, with the exception of employees of the Promoter, their immediate families and anyone else connected with this promotion. Entries from entrants under the age of 13 years must be made by a parent/guardian on their behalf.
3. The Promoter accepts no responsibility for any entries that are incomplete, illegal or fail to reach the promoter for any reason. Proof of sending is not proof of receipt. Entries via agents or third parties are invalid.
4. Only one entry per person. No entrant may receive more than one slipcase.
5. To enter, fill in your details on the entry form and send along with original sales receipt(s) showing purchase of two Doctor Who: The Darksmith Legacy books to: Doctor Who Slipcase Offer, Brands and Licensing, 80 Strand, London, WC2R 0RL.
6. The first 500 correctly completed entries will receive a slipcase.
7. Offer only available on purchases of Doctor Who: The Darksmith Legacy books.
8. Please allow 31days for receipt of your slip case.
9. Slip cases are subject to availability. In the event of exceptional circumstances, the Promoter reserves the right to amend or foreclose the promotion without notice. No correspondence will be entered into.
10. All instructions given on the entry form, form part of the terms and conditions.
11. The Promoter will use any data submitted by entrants for only the purposes of running the promotion, unless otherwise stated in the entry details. By entering this promotion, all entrants consent to the use of their personal data by the Promoter for the purposes of the administration of this promotion and any other purposes to which the entrant has consented.
12. By entering this promotion, each entrant agrees to be bound by these terms and conditions.
13. The Promoter is Penguin Books Limited, 80 Strand, London WC2R 0RL.

Cut Here

Doctor Who Slipcase Offer

Brands and Licensing

80 Strand

London

WC2R 0RL